The World Of ODYSSEUS

Written by
Neil Grant

Illustrated by
Duncan Larg, David Pentland, Carole Connelly and Eric Smith

Designed by
Keith Crawford

Edited by
Lisa Hyde

Contents

BBC

The Wooden Horse

The story of the Trojan War is one of the oldest stories in Europe. It began when Paris, son of King Priam of Troy, took a beautiful woman, Helen, to be his wife. The trouble was that Helen was married already. Her husband was the Greek king of Sparta, Menelaus.

To get Helen back, Menelaus asked for help from his brother, Agamemnon, king of Mycenae, the most powerful state in Greece, and from the other Greek princes. Some of them, like Odysseus of Ithaca, were not eager to go and fight the Trojans, whose city lay across the sea. But it was difficult to refuse. Years before, when the Greek princes were arguing about who should marry the beautiful Helen, they had all sworn to support the lucky man, whoever he was, who should win Helen's hand. Agamemnon now reminded them of their promise to Menelaus. So they collected their weapons, kissed their wives and children goodbye and sailed away to Troy.

For nearly ten years the Greeks laid siege to the city of Troy. During that time many were killed on both sides: Achilles, the greatest Greek warrior; Hector, the champion of Troy; even his brother, Paris, who had stolen Helen. Still the Greeks could not break down the walls of Troy.

If battles cannot be won by bravery and strength, they can sometimes be won by cleverness and trickery. It was Odysseus, most cunning of the Greek heroes, who thought of the Wooden Horse. But it was Epeius, the skilful ship's carpenter, who made it.

The horse was enormous. It was also hollow. In its body was a cleverly concealed trapdoor. There was room inside for thirty men to hide.

When the horse was finished the Greeks put Odysseus' plan into action. They burned down the camp where they had lived for so many years, boarded their ships and sailed away. The great Wooden Horse stood alone on the empty camp site, but Odysseus and thirty men were inside it.

When the Trojans discovered the Greeks had gone they were amazed. They flung open the gates of the city and ran down to the shore. There they found the Wooden Horse. What was it?

The Wooden Horse is inside the walls of Troy and as the city sleeps the Greeks creep out of their hiding place.

The Trojans were suspicious. It could be some kind of trap.

One Greek, named Sinon, had been left behind. The story he told the Trojans was that he had run away because Odysseus was going to have him killed. The truth, of course, was different. Sinon was really Odysseus' agent.

The Trojans asked Sinon about the horse. He told them the Greeks had made it as a gift to the goddess Athene, and the reason it was so big was to prevent the Trojans taking it into Troy. If the Wooden Horse entered Troy, said Sinon, it would mean that the Trojans would conquer all of Greece.

Nearly everyone wanted to drag the horse into the city, but a few doubted Sinon's story. Laocoon, a Trojan priest, warned that the horse was a trick. The others would not listen. 'At least look inside,' he said, and hurled his spear at the horse. The point of the spear went through the wood and grazed the neck of Perimedes, one of Odysseus' men inside. Luckily for the Greeks he did not make a sound.

At that moment, two huge serpents came out of the sea. They seized Laocoon and his two sons and crushed them to death. To the Trojans this was a sign that the Wooden Horse was guarded by the gods. Laocoon had been punished for daring to throw his spear at it. They dragged the horse into the city. That night the Trojans celebrated the end of the long siege. They drank plenty of wine and they slept well, safe at last

from Greek attack. But in the silent city the Greek Sinon climbed up to the city wall and lit a torch. An answering light came from far out at sea.

The Greek fleet had not sailed off home. They had merely sailed out of sight of Troy. Now they were coming back. Sinon made his way to the Wooden Horse and opened the trapdoor. Odysseus and his men climbed down. The trick had worked. They made their way to the city gates and pulled up the great beams which held them shut. Slowly the big gates swung open. Agamemnon was already leading the Greeks up from the beach.

The last battle of the Trojan War was soon over. The sleeping Trojans never had a chance. King Priam was killed in his palace. All the other Trojan warriors died and the victorious Greeks destroyed the city. Menelaus led Helen down to his ship while the soldiers cheered Odysseus, whose clever plan had brought them victory.

The Greek princes prepared to sail home, this time in earnest. But for many of them home was farther away than they thought. Odysseus, for example, would not reach Ithaca, where his wife Penelope was waiting for him, until another ten years had passed. Many strange adventures lay before him. He would meet horrible monsters and overcome terrible dangers. He would have to fight against the anger of gods and the magic of sorcerers. These are the adventures related in the *Odyssey*.

Homer and the Greeks

The story of the Trojan War and the story of Odysseus' adventures were told by the poet Homer, who lived between 750 and 700 BC.

That was before the great age of Classical Greek civilisation, when the famous temples were built and the great philosophers, playwrights and artists were at work. To the people of the Classical age Homer was a writer of the distant past, as Shakespeare is to us.

They probably did not know much more about Homer than we do, which is very little. There is a legend that he was blind and many scholars today believe that he was not one writer but two, or even more!

Homer was writing about a time much earlier still. The people in his stories, whom we call Greeks, are great kings and warriors. Their homes are palaces, their plates are gold and their deeds are tremendous. They are heroes belonging to a Heroic Age which existed (so the Greeks of Homer's time believed) in the distant past.

Was there a Heroic Age when gods took part in human battles and heroes fought monsters and magicians? No! Yet, about 500 years before Homer's time, a rich and powerful civilisation *did* exist in Greece. We call it Mycenaean, because Mycenae was its greatest city.

The Mycenaeans were not a single nation: each city was a separate state with its own king. But they were united by their language (Greek) and their way of life.

Around 1200 BC the Mycenaean civilisation was destroyed. No one knows how or why. There followed a time we now call the Dark Age. Civilisation almost vanished, and people even forgot how to read and write.

Yet the Mycenaeans were not forgotten completely. Stories were told of the great heroes who had lived in Mycenae, Sparta and other cities, although the cities themselves had disappeared (archaeologists rediscovered them about 100 years ago).

These stories were handed down, from parents to children, for about 500 years.

They became fairy stories full of gods, monsters and superheroes.

When people learned how to write again, the stories were written down. This happened in Homer's time, or very soon after. Homer, who stands at the beginning of Greek literature, also stands at the end of a long line of Greek story-tellers. His books, the *Iliad* (about the Trojan War) and the *Odyssey* (about Odysseus' travels), which became a sort of Bible for the Greeks, are the latest version of ancient stories which had been passed down by the people of the Dark Age.

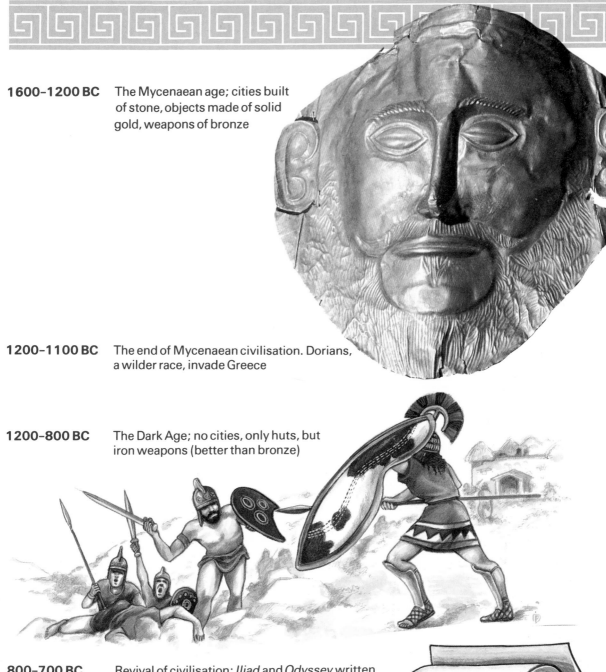

1600–1200 BC   The Mycenaean age; cities built of stone, objects made of solid gold, weapons of bronze

1200–1100 BC   The end of Mycenaean civilisation. Dorians, a wilder race, invade Greece

1200–800 BC   The Dark Age; no cities, only huts, but iron weapons (better than bronze)

800–700 BC   Revival of civilisation; *Iliad* and *Odyssey* written

700–500 BC

Archaic period;
Greek art developing

500–300 BC

Classical period;
Greek civilisation at
its height

The Odyssey

The *Odyssey* tells of the adventures of Odysseus after the end of the Trojan War. Many of these adventures are folk tales, like the folk tales of later times about witches, giants and magic goings-on. Others are more realistic. Part of the *Odyssey* is about what happened after Odysseus had reached Ithaca: how he got rid of the unpleasant young men who had taken over his palace and were trying to take his wife from him as well. It's an exciting story and it could have

happened exactly as Homer tells it. Homer was a poet and story-teller, but he was not a historian. To ask how much of what Homer wrote is true is, in a way, a silly question because we can never know. But it is an interesting question all the same.

Until just over 100 years ago no one knew if the city of Troy had ever existed because most people thought the whole story of the Trojan War was imaginary. But in the 1870s the remains of Troy

Part of a building excavated by Schliemann in Mycenae.

were discovered by a famous archaeologist, Heinrich Schliemann. In fact he discovered several cities whose remains lay in layers, one on top of another, below the ground. One of these cities had existed at the time of Homer's Trojan War. What's more, it had been violently destroyed at just about the time Homer said it had!

We now know that there really was a Trojan War. (It was probably not fought over a woman, even a woman as beautiful as Helen. It's more likely it was the result of a quarrel over trade.)

We no longer suppose that Homer's stories are only fairy tales. There certainly was a Trojan War, so there may have been a Wooden Horse. There may have been kings called Agamemnon, Menelaus and Priam. But a more important question is: What did Homer's readers think about the *Iliad* and the *Odyssey*?

They probably believed in Homer in the way that some people today believe in the Christian Bible. While some would think that every word was true, others would think it was all a fairy tale.

A diagram showing how archaeologists find objects in the earth – the deeper the layer, the older the object.

A lion hunt dagger discovered by Schliemann at Mycenae in 1876.

Was there a real king of Ithaca called Odysseus? We can never know, but we may guess that there was because the hero of Homer's *Odyssey* seems such a real person. He is certainly more human than other ancient heroes.

At first sight he did not look much like a hero, because he was not very tall. When he stood up to make a speech he was not such a grand figure of a man as Agamemnon or Menelaus. But when he began to speak he was much more impressive. All Greek princes were taught the art of public speaking as part of their education and Odysseus was the best speaker among the heroes at Troy.

Odysseus was less proud, less high and mighty, than other heroes. His kingdom was a small, faraway island and his ancestors were not very distinguished, but they were remarkable. This was an important matter to the Greeks. Who you were depended on who your ancestors were. It is true that Odysseus counted Zeus (king of the gods) as one of his ancestors. But that was common, almost necessary. Any Greek hero worth his salt was descended from Zeus and usually from several other gods and goddesses as well.

Though not tall, he was broad and strong. Marching among his men, someone said, he looked like a ram among sheep. His hair was reddish (a common colour among the Greeks) but his beard was dark.

He was not such a mighty warrior as Achilles, but he was a brave fighter. In his last great battle, against the men who had taken over his palace in Ithaca, he killed them with arrows from a bow no one else was strong enough to draw. Odysseus' greatest qualities were his cunning and intelligence. He was the cleverest of the Greeks, the man they always called on to get them out of a difficult spot. It had to be Odysseus who thought of the Wooden Horse, or of escaping from Polyphemus' cave by clinging to the belly of a sheep. Heroes were not usually this crafty. They almost despised cleverness. If Achilles had been still alive he would probably have said that the Wooden Horse was a sneaky trick.

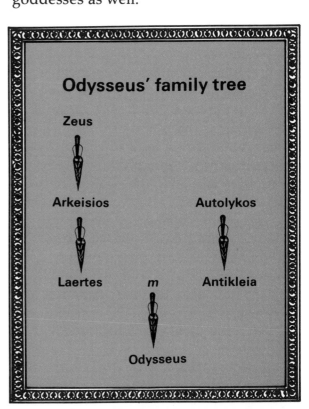

Odysseus' family tree

Zeus

Arkeisios   Autolykos

Laertes   *m*   Antikleia

Odysseus

On his father's side Odysseus was descended from Zeus, but there was no long list of famous ancestors in between, as in the family trees of other Greek heroes. One of his grandparents, Autolykos, was quite famous, but not for heroic reasons. He was a well-known cattle thief! Perhaps it was from him that Odysseus inherited his cunning.

Where did Odysseus go?

The *Odyssey* is a story, not history. But like many stories it may be related to real events. It may have begun, 500 years before Homer, with memories of a 'real' Odysseus who sailed around the Mediterranean after the fall of Troy. We can recognise some of the places that Odysseus visited, and we can make a good guess at others.

When the Greeks sailed away from Troy the ships were scattered by a storm. Odysseus and his twelve ships were driven north to Ismarus, a town in Thrace (modern Bulgaria). Leaving that coast they sailed south, meaning to go round Greece to Ithaca, which is on the opposite coast, but they were driven too far south and reached the Land of the Lotus Eaters on the North African coast, probably the island of Jerba, off Libya.

Sailing north again, they came to the big island where the Cyclops lived. This could only be Sicily. After escaping from Polyphemus, they were sailing peacefully homeward when Odysseus' men foolishly opened the bag which contained all the winds. (It had been given to Odysseus by Aeolus, king of the winds, at the island of Ustica.) The gales that escaped from the bag drove them backwards into unknown seas, until they landed in the country of the Laestrygonians.

At this point a mist descends on the Mediterranean. The Laestrygonians could have lived in several places. Homer's description of the harbour makes Bonifacio, on the south coast of Corsica, a likely guess. Other traditions say that the Laestrygonians lived in Italy.

Odysseus escaped from there with only one ship, which came to Circe's island. This must surely have been the modern Monte Circeo, on the Italian coast, although it is not an island (there is a peninsula, which could easily be mistaken for an island). By now Odysseus was thoroughly lost. He told Circe, 'East and west mean nothing to us here'.

Perhaps this explains why Odysseus next sailed due west, in the opposite direction from Greece. The Pillars of Hercules, named after another Greek hero, are at the western end of the Mediterranean and it seems unlikely that the 'real' Odysseus would have sailed there. These were unknown waters even in Homer's time. However, it was there that Odysseus had to go in order to enter the Underworld, as Circe advised.

After returning to Circe's island, Odysseus passed the Sirens, on an island off the south-west coast of Italy, and sailed through the Messina Strait, between Scylla and Charybdis. All the experts agree about this stage.

All was going well until Odysseus' men, hungry for meat, killed the cattle of the Sun God, somewhere on the east coast of Sicily. (The east coast of Sicily is quite different from the west and Odysseus would not have realised it was the same island as the island of the Cyclops.) The Sun God soon had his revenge. The ship was wrecked and all were drowned – except Odysseus, who made himself a raft from the wreckage and was eventually washed up on the island of the beautiful nymph Calypso. Old tradition says that this was Ceuta, the island opposite Gibraltar. But Odysseus could never have drifted so far. The current would have carried him south from Sicily, so Calypso's island could well have been Malta.

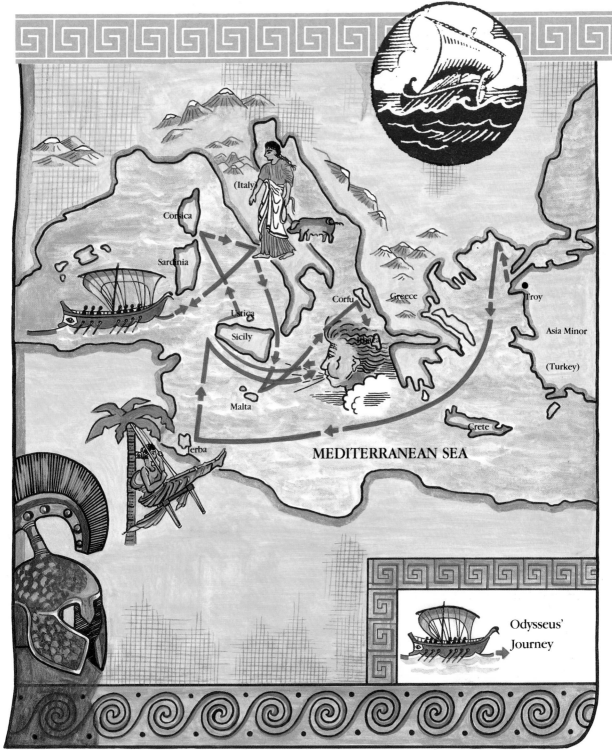

Odysseus spent seven years with Calypso, but at last the goddess Athene took a hand and asked Zeus to make Calypso let her captive go. He made a boat and set sail, only to be wrecked again by the bad-tempered Poseidon off the Land of the Phaeacians – the first real humans he had met for a long time. He was now in home waters, for the Land of the Phaeacians was probably the Greek island of Corfu, not far from Ithaca. After he had been well looked after by the Phaeacians he made his final voyage in one of their ships, landing at last on his own island of Ithaca. It had taken him ten years to get home from Troy.

Religion and the gods

The Greeks had a great many gods and goddesses. They thought of them as creatures much like human beings. They looked like people, and they behaved like people. They ate and drank, got married and had children, lost their tempers, fell in love and did everything that human beings do.

But they were gods all the same. They did not grow old and they did not die. They had supernatural powers. They could, if they wanted, turn themselves into animals.

Most of them had special jobs. Hephaestos, for example, was not only the god of blacksmiths (a very important craft then) but a blacksmith himself. Artemis was the goddess of hunting, Aphrodite the goddess of love and Ares the god of war.

All the gods and goddesses took part in human affairs. Sometimes they were helpful, sometimes they were cruel. During the Trojan War the gods were divided, some supporting the Greeks, some the Trojans.

Although there were no great temples in Homer's time, the gods were worshipped in sanctuaries. These were simple enclosures with an altar, perhaps a small, simple building and often a sacred tree. People gave gifts and made sacrifices to the gods thinking that they gave talent and luck to mankind. The gods might behave foolishly, like people, but they had to be taken seriously. It was unwise to mock the gods. A person who showed lack of respect soon came to a sticky end.

Religion was part of everyday life. Men seldom did anything without thinking of its religious effects. Would the gods be pleased? Because people did not know scientific reasons for ordinary events, like a thunderstorm or a waterfall, they invented a religious explanation. Thunder, they said, was caused by Zeus throwing his spear.

To the Greeks the whole world was a living thing. The ocean was not only the ocean; it was also 'Ocean', who was a vague kind of being (he had a wife) as well as a force of nature. The Earth itself was called Gaia and was a female. A stone, an island, a river – everything in nature was alive. When Odysseus arrived off the rocky coast of the island of the Phaeacians, he prayed to a river which entered the sea there so that it would allow him to swim ashore.

Priests

There were priests in Homer's time, though they were nothing like the modern kinds of priest. Their job was to look after the sanctuaries, the sacrifices and the prayers. But they were no more religious than people in other jobs, because the gods were everywhere.

When people wanted to know the gods' opinion of anything, they asked an oracle or soothsayer, a kind of priest, who was expert in interpreting the 'signs', like the sea serpent which killed Laocoon or the fighting eagles which appeared at Ithaca to foretell the vengeance of Odysseus.

Among the many gods and goddesses of the Greeks, four played important parts in the *Odyssey*.

Poseidon was the brother of Zeus, although they were not always on good terms. He ruled the sea, as Zeus ruled the land and sky. The Greeks pictured him rather like Zeus, but wilder and rougher, just as the sea is wilder than the land. He carried a spear with three points, called a trident, like the spear used by tuna fishermen.

Sea-faring people naturally tried to keep on the right side of Poseidon. Odysseus' troubles really began after he had made Poseidon furious by blinding Polyphemus. That hideous, one-eyed giant was Poseidon's son. Although sons of Zeus were usually heroes, sons of Poseidon often turned out to be evil and violent.

The ill-will of Poseidon would surely have put an end to Odysseus if he had not been supported by an equally powerful goddess, **Athene**. She, with Penelope (Odysseus' wife), is the heroine of the *Odyssey*. She often arrives on the scene, disguised as a human being, just in time to save Odysseus. Athene was the daughter of Zeus, and was born out of his head dressed in

The first was **Zeus**, king of the gods. The Greeks pictured him as a powerful, bearded man in the prime of life, no longer young but not yet old. He was terrifying when angry and hurled his spear or thunderbolt.

Zeus had supreme power over other gods, and he could do things that they could not. Only Zeus could order the nymph Calypso, who was a kind of goddess herself, to let Odysseus leave the island where she held him prisoner. Zeus often interfered in human affairs, sometimes at the request of other gods. He was very fond of pretty women, and he had love affairs with many human women. As a result, many Greek heroes could claim Zeus as an ancestor.

armour. As you would expect after such an impressive start in life, she proved to be a very powerful goddess. She was warlike but also beautiful and, more important, wise. She was the goddess of reason and was worshipped by philosophers, artists and poets. It is not surprising she admired Odysseus because he was, like her, both a warrior and a thinker.

Hermes also helped Odysseus. He showed him how to break the spell of Circe, after she had bewitched his companions, and he carried Zeus' order for Calypso to release Odysseus.

It was Hermes' special task to be a messenger of Zeus, and of the other gods. He moved about the world speedily, thanks to the wings on his sandals and helmet. He too was a son of Zeus. The Greeks pictured him as a very young man, almost a boy.

Apollo

Athene

Ares

The chief gods and goddesses

Aphrodite (Roman name Venus). Goddess of love, born from the ocean.

Apollo (Apollo). The sun god, also a hunter and musician. Son of Zeus, he was portrayed as a very handsome young man.

Ares (Mars). The god of war, son of Zeus and Hera. He was rather violent and unreliable.

Artemis (Diana). The goddess of hunting and the moon, twin sister of Apollo.

Athene (Minerva). The goddess of wisdom and warfare.

Demeter (Ceres). The goddess of farming and the sister of Zeus.

Dionysos (Bacchus). The god of wine, dancing and the drama, a son of Zeus.

Hades (Pluto). The king of the Underworld. He was a grim, frightening god and a brother of Zeus and Poseidon.

Hephaestos (Vulcan). The blacksmith, a god of fire. He was a son of Hera and was rather dim and unlucky, in spite of being married to Aphrodite.

Hera (Juno). Wife of Zeus.

Hermes (Mercury). The messenger god.

Poseidon (Neptune). The king of the sea.

Zeus (Jupiter). The king of the gods, the land and the sky.

Hades

Dionysos

Hermes

Aphrodite

Heroes

Besides the gods and goddesses the Greeks also respected, and even worshipped, the ancient heroes of legend.

The heroes were less than gods, but more than men. Homer's heroes are, as a rule, princes descended from a long line of famous ancestors, and among their ancestors are gods and goddesses. They are men of extraordinary courage and strength and sometimes wisdom.

The heroes lived in a time when gods and men often mingled – a time of legend, not history.

The most popular adventure of Theseus was killing the Minotaur, a bull-headed creature which lived in a labyrinth (an underground maze) in Crete and ate boys and girls for breakfast. Theseus is supposed to have lived shortly before the Trojan War and the stories about him may have been based on memories of a real hero. All these mythical heroes were older than Odysseus and the champions of the Trojan War.

Heroes were important to the Greeks in much the same way as their ancestors were. Sometimes their ancestors *were* heroes. They offered prayers and sacrifices to them as well as to the gods, and often an animal was slaughtered and placed on an altar as an offering. In the *Iliad* Homer tells of a sacrifice offered by Odysseus to the god Apollo when 100 cattle were slaughtered. Usually one ox was enough!

The heroes acted as a link between men and gods. Ordinary people, when they died, became ghosts. But heroes, although they also 'died', kept the same qualities after death which they had when alive. They were able to speak to the gods on behalf of human beings and sometimes became minor gods themselves.

In some ways the ancient hero was like a modern hero, such as Superman or Dr Who, because both have magic powers which ordinary people would like to have themselves. But the Greek heroes were usually regarded with respect and reverence, while Superman and Dr Who are figures of entertainment.

The typical Greek hero, like the mighty Heracles, was a man of enormous strength and courage, but his muscles often seemed to be bigger than his brain.

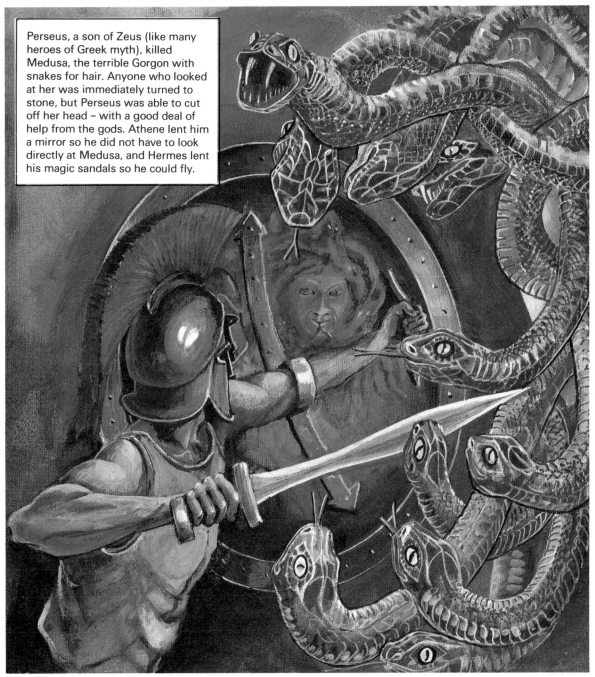

Perseus, a son of Zeus (like many heroes of Greek myth), killed Medusa, the terrible Gorgon with snakes for hair. Anyone who looked at her was immediately turned to stone, but Perseus was able to cut off her head – with a good deal of help from the gods. Athene lent him a mirror so he did not have to look directly at Medusa, and Hermes lent his magic sandals so he could fly.

Odysseus is rather different. He is certainly strong and brave, but his greatest quality is his cleverness. Although he talks to gods and fights monsters he seems more like a normal human being than the older heroes like Heracles.

Odysseus is really the last of the Greek heroes. Heracles had hundreds of descendants but Odysseus had none, except his son Telemachus. The Age of Heroes came to an end with his death. After that there were no more legends and the gods no longer came down from Mount Olympus to mix with human beings. The time of legends was over and history had begun.

Monsters

Like all good heroes, Odysseus had to overcome terrible monsters during his travels. Prehistoric people lived in a dangerous world. They could not understand the causes of disasters like floods or earthquakes and because they believed that everything in nature was alive, they imagined evil creatures of some sort were responsible.

In fact, they thought that earthquakes were caused by a race of giants who lived deep in the earth. The **Cyclops** may have been related to those underground giants. However, by the time of the *Odyssey* they had become shepherds. But shepherds of a very unusual kind! They were enormous, savage creatures with a single eye in the middle of their foreheads. They lived in caves in Sicily or southern Italy and had no possessions except their flocks of sheep. They preferred human flesh to mutton, however.

Odysseus and his companions were trapped in the cave of the one-eyed giant Polyphemus. Odysseus made him drunk and put his eye out with a stake. In the morning, when Polyphemus let his sheep out to graze, he felt their backs to make sure the Greeks were not escaping with them. But Odysseus and his men were holding on underneath.

Odysseus makes his getaway as a furious Polyphemus displays his rage.

The **Laestrygonians** were also man-eating giants. Odysseus and his men arrived at their country by chance, when the wind blew his ships there. The giants gathered on the cliffs and hurled rocks at the Greek ships anchored in the harbour. Every ship was sunk except the ship of Odysseus, who managed to escape. The rest of his men swam ashore, only to be eaten by the Laestrygonians.

The **Sirens** were another kind of danger but this time Odysseus knew about them in advance, having been warned by Circe. The Sirens were wonderful singers and musicians who lived on a small island in the Mediterranean. The mysterious beauty of their singing attracted passing sailors. So powerful was the attraction of their music that no one could resist it. But when a ship came near, it was wrecked on the rocky coast, and the sailors were eaten by the Sirens.

On Circe's advice, Odysseus made his men block their ears with wax so they could not hear the dangerous song of the Sirens. But Odysseus himself, being a man with a lively and curious mind, wanted to listen. He told his men to tie him to the mast and not to release him no matter how hard he begged. The Sirens were so angry when Odysseus' ship sailed straight on past that they threw themselves into the sea and were drowned.

Later stories about the Sirens say that they were extremely beautiful women, and attracted sailors by their looks rather than their music. From those stories we get the modern meaning of 'siren': a woman who sets out to attract men through her physical appeal. Homer says nothing about that. In the *Odyssey*, the two Sirens (later stories say there were three or four) are half woman and half bird.

Scylla and Charybdis were monsters of different kinds who worked together. Charybdis was a sea monster. Three times a day she drank a huge amount of sea water, and anything that was floating on the surface was sucked down and swallowed. In other words, Charybdis was a whirlpool. A tiny whirlpool is created when the plug is pulled out of the bath. Large whirlpools in the seas are most often found in a narrow strait between two coasts. Charybdis lived in just such a strait, the Messina Strait, between Sicily and Italy.

Scylla lived opposite, in a cave on the shore. She had the form of a woman, but around her body grew six dogs' heads. When anyone came close enough to the shore the dogs' heads darted out of the cave and pounced on them.

Charybdis can be explained as a whirlpool. What, then, was Scylla? She was probably a dangerous rock off the shore, on which many ships had been wrecked through trying to avoid the whirlpool. There is more than one place on the coast of Sicily which could have been Scylla, and there is still, to this day, a village near that coast called Scilla. A ship that steered clear of Charybdis would be attacked by Scylla. One that gave Scylla a wide berth would be sucked down by Charybdis. Odysseus chose to sail nearer Scylla. He lost six men to the six dogs' heads, but the rest came through safely.

22

Ithaca

Odysseus was the king of Ithaca, an island off the west coast of Greece. His kingdom was small and not very important. Most of the other Greek heroes of the Trojan War came from larger and richer kingdoms on the mainland. They probably looked on Odysseus in his poor, out-of-the-way island, as a country cousin.

Odysseus may have hidden his treasure in a mysterious cave like this one.

Odysseus' kingdom was made up of three islands, and he also had some land on the coast of mainland Greece where he grazed his cattle. Ithaca is the smallest of the three islands, but it is in the best position to control shipping routes. That is probably why it contained the capital.

Odysseus himself described Ithaca as a rocky and rugged island, mountainous and woody. Today most of the woods, except for olive trees, have gone. As in the rest of Greece, the grazing of goats has prevented young trees growing. Otherwise Odysseus' description fits the modern island, called Itháki or Thiáki. Homer may have visited Ithaca himself, since he describes it so well. In the *Odyssey*, when Odysseus finally returned to Ithaca at the end of his travels, he hid his treasure in a cave. The cave is described in detail by Homer. In the same bay where Odysseus is supposed to have landed, there is to this day a cave which could easily be the cave that Homer described over 2700 years ago.

Life has not changed a great deal on Ithaca even in all that time. There are no factories, no sprawling supermarkets and no soaring skyscrapers. Until about 100 years ago, there weren't any roads. Other places in the *Odyssey* can still be recognised. The house of Eumaeus, Odysseus' loyal pig-keeper, was close to 'Raven's Crag' and 'Arethusa's Fountain'. There is a line of cliffs where ravens nest that is still called Raven's Crag by the people of Ithaca, and close by is a freshwater spring which fills a pool among the rocks.

In the northern part of the island is a place called Polis, which means 'city' or 'state'. Archaeologists have found remains in the same area which date from the Mycenaean period – the Age of the Heroes. Was Odysseus' palace here? It seems likely, but no one has found any trace of it – yet.

The sunset over the beautiful island of Ithaca.

The Greek ships that sailed to make war on Troy were not a proper fleet or navy. No such thing existed. Nor were there trained sailors in Homer's Greece. It was a part-time job. Nearly every man was a sailor of sorts and most men worked a boat at some time in their lives.

Only a rich man could afford to build a ship. When he had built it he was expected to let the city, or state, use it if required. The state then provided a crew and the owner sailed as captain, taking a large share of the profits of the voyage. Sensible people went to sea only at certain seasons. It was usually safe for a short time in the spring, but the chief sailing season was the summer, late June to August, when winds were reliable and storms unlikely. At other times long voyages were risky. No one sailed at night unless he had to. Before the sun set the ship made for shore.

Many voyages were very short. A farmer who wished to sell his crops in the next region would carry them down the valleys to the sea, and then sail up the coast. That was easier than crossing the mountains. Merchants sometimes sailed much farther. They went to Egypt to buy corn and wine. They sailed in convoys to the Black Sea and to north-west Italy (via the Strait of Messina) to fetch metals needed to make bronze.

A sea-faring life was exciting and dangerous – and the dangers were not all due to nature. Any man might take to the life of a trader for a year or two, hoping to make his fortune. He might grow rich by honest trade or he might find piracy more profitable. There wasn't much difference! At one time in Ithaca, Odysseus pretended to be a nobleman's son from Crete who said he had taken part in many 'foreign adventures'. That meant raiding foreign towns or capturing foreign ships. Honourable men saw nothing wrong in that. They often boasted about it, as Odysseus did. Even ordinary merchant ships had weapons, and if the chance of a raid came up they took it. Pirates would also take part in honest trade. Merchant, pirate, pirate, merchant – they were very much the same.

Although the Greeks were a sea-faring people they were not fond of fish. When Odysseus' men ran out of meat, they ate up all the ship's stores down to the last grain of flour. Only when they were starving did they set out to catch some fish. Fishing was a very lowly occupation and as food fish was fit for only the most wretched people!

Detail of a bronze statue of Poseidon, the god of the sea.

Odysseus' ship

The ship in which Odysseus sailed the Mediterranean for so many years was a simple craft, but strong and seaworthy. It was not unlike the ships of the Vikings, many centuries later, which were good enough to cross the stormy Atlantic.

It was an open boat with no proper deck or cabin, although it probably had sections at the bow and stern which were partly enclosed. When the sail was lowered it could act as a shelter against rain or sun.

The ship had a single mast of pinewood and a square sail made of linen or papyrus. This type of sail is fine when the wind is behind you but not much good when it isn't, so the ship also needed oars. There were probably about twenty oars, ten a side, held in loops of leather. The rowers sat on benches. Running before the wind the ship could sail at about six knots (eleven kilometres an hour).

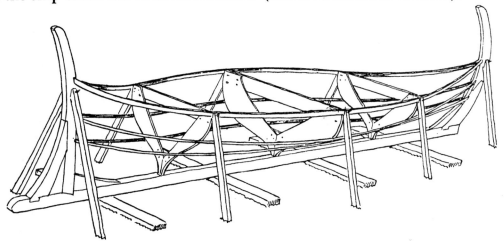

The rudder had not been invented yet, but the ship could be steered with a large oar at the stern. As the wooden hull had no keel, it rocked about whenever the sea was the least bit rough. But the lack of a keel had some advantages: the ship could enter very shallow water, and it could be easily run up on a beach. If it had to be anchored in open water, a big stone was used as an anchor.

In such a small and clumsy craft storms, rocks, whirlpools and currents, which would not be noticed in a modern ship, were terrifying menaces. Odysseus was in a strange, mysterious world. It was easy to imagine that dreadful monsters lay in wait to destroy him. He had no charts or instruments to guide him, not even a compass. Whenever he could he

sailed close to land. If a storm blew up he could run the ship ashore and wait for it to pass.

Of course Odysseus knew the sea well. He was, after all, an islander, and he had been a merchant (as well as a pirate!). He probably knew the sea as well as anyone. When it came to navigation he was far from helpless even when land was out of sight. He knew that the sun came up in the east and went down in the west. At night, if the stars were out, he could tell which direction was north by the Pole Star. He was the first sailor we know who navigated by the stars.

In Odysseus' time ships were not given names, but Homer often describes ships as 'black'. This probably means they were coated with tar to preserve the wood.

A Greek helmet
in bronze,
dedicated to Zeus.

The warrior Achilles taunts
the Trojans from his chariot.

The Mycenaeans lived in the Bronze Age. They made metal objects out of bronze, which is a mixture of copper and tin. By Homer's time the Greeks had learned to smelt iron, which is a harder metal than bronze and makes better weapons. In the *Odyssey* the Greeks wear bronze armour and use bronze weapons, but sometimes iron is mentioned too.

The Greeks wore armour in battle, but not a complete suit of armour like medieval knights. Their helmets were very impressive, with high crests and sometimes a long plume of horsehair. A strip of bronze came down in front of the face to cover the nose and cheeks, creating a very fierce appearance. Athene, being a goddess, wore a gold helmet.

The body was protected from the shoulders to below the waist by a fitted cuirass or corselet, which left arms and legs free. Greaves of thin metal, made to grip the leg, guarded the knees and shins. A round shield was carried on the left arm.

The chief weapons were a spear and a short sword, and sometimes a bow and arrows. Odysseus was a formidable archer whose mighty bow could not be bent by others. (He left it at home, however, perhaps because the sea air would have spoiled it.)

The Greeks also fought from horse-drawn chariots, the forerunner of the tank. They were then a new weapon in the Mediterranean region. After he had killed Hector, Achilles dragged his body behind his chariot around the walls of Troy.

Soldiers were well armed for a battle in the open, but they could do very little against a city guarded by stone walls. Troy was conquered, after all, by a trick.

In a battle, the chariots were placed in front and the foot soldiers behind. Anyone suspected of being a coward was put in the middle, where he couldn't run away. Tactics were simple, to say the least. The chariots rushed about to create disorder among the enemy and the battle ended up as a series of man-to-man fights. A famous warrior was simply a man who was brave and strong in a fight. He did not have to plan strategy and tactics like a modern general.

Bows were made of wood with strips of horn on the inside and layers of animal sinew on the outside, bound with leather. To string the bow you had to bend it backwards, making it curve in the opposite direction. This is how Odysseus strung his bow after his opponents had failed to do it.

The Greeks at home

Odysseus and the other famous heroes of the Trojan War are called kings, but they were not great monarchs who ruled over large countries. They had a few thousand subjects at the most and their kingdoms were smaller than a modern city. We should think of a man like Odysseus as something like the chief of a tribe, and although life in a Greek kingdom was more complicated than life in a tribe, there was no organised government and no system of laws. Life was simple and hard.

The main living room in a Mycenean Palace.

Odysseus may have been a king but he was not too grand to plough his own fields, nor to take part in trade as a merchant. He was also, it seems, a capable do-it-yourself man. We hear of him building a bedroom as an extension to his palace in Ithaca, although that may not mean he built it with his own hands. The most important people in the kingdom were the king and his family, especially his eldest son, who would be the next king. Below the royal family, though not far below them, came the nobility. Most of them were related to the king, or at least claimed to have the same ancestors.

The royal and noble families formed a clan, people united by blood and loyalty, and in effect this clan *was* the kingdom. They owned most of the land, and they controlled the rest of the people. Nearly all the Greeks – and certainly all the Greek heroes – whom we meet in the *Odyssey* belonged to the aristocratic

upper class.

Ordinary people, such as potters, herdsmen, fishermen and servants (including slaves, who were often prisoners of war), had little power or property. They hardly appear in the *Odyssey*. It is true that Odysseus' most loyal friend in Ithaca, Eumaeus, was a pig-keeper. But he was also the son of a king. Homer does not say why a king's son was working as a pig-keeper, but it can't have been common!

The men who sailed with Odysseus belonged to the aristocratic clan. Although the Greeks had professional, full-time soldiers, they did not have trained sailors. Odysseus was the captain of his ship and he gave the orders, but he called his crew his comrades. They were also warriors and land-owners; sailoring was something they learned to do when necessary, like learning to drive a car today.

There are no pictures of people from Homer's time, and although he describes armour in great detail he does not say much about ordinary clothes. However, in the world's museums are many ancient pots painted with human figures which were made within about 200 years of Homer's time.

The Greeks wore simple, home-made clothes. A woman's dress was simply a large piece of material arranged in folds and fastened with clasps on the shoulders to form a tunic. Homer often describes a pretty woman as 'white-armed'. That does not mean her arms were any whiter than the rest of her, only that the arms were left bare. Except for the head and feet, everything else was covered.

On special occasions such as religious festivals ladies of high rank wore a very fine robe, which was embroidered. The goddess Athene once made such a robe for Hera, the wife of Zeus.

Men wore home-made tunics like the women's. In cold weather a cloak or mantle, fastened at the throat, went on top. Waterproof capes were made out of vellum – the skin of lambs or kids. Both men and women wore leather sandals although some 'sandals' were more like boots, covering feet and ankles.

Hats were not much in fashion. Women covered their heads with a shawl or a fold of their tunic. Heroes appear on painted pots in their splendid helmets, but Odysseus is often shown wearing a cone-shaped hat called a *pilos*.

Clothes were made by the women of the family. Not only did they make the clothes, they made the cloth too (there wasn't much cutting and stitching needed). Odysseus' wife Penelope spent the evenings while he was away at her loom, weaving yarn into cloth. Everyday clothes were the natural colour of the wool. Very fine robes, for royalty only, were sometimes dyed purple, with a dye obtained from a certain kind of shellfish. Tens of thousands of shellfish were needed for enough dye to colour one robe. Ordinary people lived in simple huts, but palaces were made of stone and richly decorated. The hall of the royal palace of the Phaeacians had walls of bronze, with a band of blue enamel decoration running around them. It had doors of gold and doorposts of silver. Furniture consisted of couches, used for eating as well as sleeping, chests for storing things and three-legged tables and stools. Bowls and basins were made of clay (pottery), bronze or, for the very rich, gold.

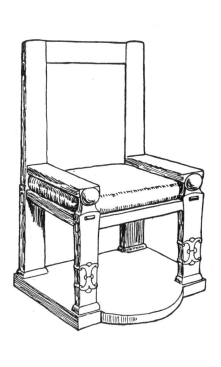

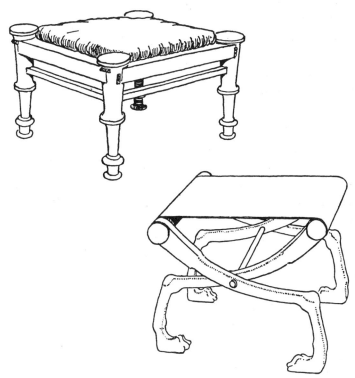

The wedding preparations of a girl called Thalea, from the fifth century.

Many of the nicest people in the *Odyssey* are women. Even Circe, who is a witch, is not so bad in the end. Nausicaa, the teenage princess of the Phaeacians who finds Odysseus shipwrecked on the beach, is a charming and realistic character. We feel we know her well. Homer liked women, that's obvious. Not every Greek writer did. Hesiod, who lived soon after Homer, disliked all women and advised men never to marry.

In Greece at that time a woman's place was at home. Men led a more exciting life. They had more freedom too, although women were far from prisoners. They could go out to religious ceremonies, to do some shopping or to visit a friend. When Odysseus met Nausicaa she had come to do the laundry in a stream far from the palace and she was playing a ball game with her attendants. Ladies did not, of course, go out alone.

Husbands and wives (who were often much younger) lived separate lives much of the time. They did not eat together, nor use the same bath nor the same bedroom. The main bedroom belonged to the husband, and his wife slept there only when he invited her. Sometimes he might even invite other girls, though most husbands were too frightened to do such a thing. Odysseus' wife, Penelope, is the model of a loyal, patient wife. To us she may seem a little *too* loyal and patient. Yet she is also a person of strong will and quick intelligence. She is almost the only person in the *Odyssey* who succeeds in tricking Odysseus, the great trickster. Although the husband was supposed to be the boss, wives could not be treated like servants. Women had rights too. If a husband treated his wife badly, he would get into serious trouble with her family. A woman's father continued to be her protector, if needed, after she was married. Fathers often felt an extra responsibility because they picked husbands for their daughters.

The most important duty of a wife was to have children, especially boys. Unwanted children were sometimes allowed to die.

A wife was also in charge of the household. If she were the wife of an important man she had many servants to help her. But in many ways house-keeping was a much bigger job then. Everything had to be done at home, including making clothes. Women had plenty to keep them busy and we do not hear that they were often bored.

Odysseus surprises the princess Nausicaa and her maids as they do the laundry.

Farming

Odysseus and his fellow princes might go voyaging or making war, they might become merchants, or shipowners or even businessmen of a kind, but they were all, without exception, landowners. It was their land and their herds of animals that made them important people.

One story about Odysseus, not in the *Odyssey*, tells of him working a plough. (He was ploughing the beach with an ox and an ass yoked together, because he wanted some visitors to think he was mad – a typical Odyssean trick!) The plough that he used had no metal blade to cut and turn the soil. It was simply a heavy spike which made deep scratches in the ground. A man followed the plough scattering seed. Sometimes the seed was covered by a boy using a mattock, a tool like a heavy hoe or a pickaxe with a broad blade.

Corn, beans and peas were the main crops. In Greece the harvest was early – in May or June. The corn was cut with a sickle, children gathered the sheaves (stalks), which were tied in bundles and taken to the threshing floor where they were trampled. Then they were winnowed – thrown up into the air so the chaff blew away while the heavier grain fell to the floor. A second harvest came in September, when the grapes were ripe.

A mouflon sheep.

Farmers also kept animals. Goats and sheep were the most common. Polyphemus and the Cyclops were good shepherds who cared for their sheep and looked after them well. That was the only nice thing that could be said about those one-eyed cannibals.

In Ithaca Eumaeus, Odysseus' pig-keeper, looked after thousands of pigs, and we also hear of herds of cattle in the *Odyssey*. Stealing cattle was a serious crime, because a man's wealth was measured by the cattle he owned. Many of Odysseus' troubles resulted from his men killing and eating the cattle of the Sun God.

Oxen were also used for ploughing, though some thought mules (half horse, half donkey) were better. Horses were kept for pulling carts or (in war) chariots, but the Greeks were not riders. They travelled mostly on foot.

It is possible to work out how many animals Odysseus owned from what Homer tells us in the *Odyssey*. The total comes to about 30 000! With herds of that size, Odysseus was a very rich man.

Treading grapes to make wine.

In Homer's Greece almost any reason would do to have a feast. Guests would be invited and an animal killed – an ox for a big party. After the meal came dancing and sporting contests, as well as quieter games like draughts. A poet might be invited to provide entertainment and Homer himself probably earned his living that way. Life was rough and simple, but except for the poor there was usually plenty to eat. Meat came from both farm and wild animals. Most meals were mainly meat and bread. The bread was baked every day in flat loaves by the women. Meat was cooked in a three-legged cauldron, but the best parts were roasted or grilled. Preparing roast meat was a man's job, and this tradition goes on still. In homes today women do the cooking but men look after the barbecue.

Pomegranates.

Orchards produced many kinds of fruit. When Odysseus was a boy he had pear and apple trees, figs and vines to look after. Pomegranates and olives grew in the orchard of the Phaeacian palace, and the Lotus Eaters of course ate the fruit of the lotus plant (rather floury).

Food was washed down with wine, and people drank a good deal of it. It was strong wine too, but it was usually first mixed with water in a big pottery jar called a krater.

Bread was served in baskets, meat on wooden or metal plates. People ate with their fingers. Wine cups too were metal, perhaps gold. Archaeologists have found some very beautiful ones in Mycenaean tombs.

In the larger houses guests – sometimes strangers – often appeared at meals. The Greeks seem to have been fond of travelling (perhaps that was why they enjoyed hearing about Odysseus' travels), and as there were no hotels or restaurants they depended on ordinary people for food (though they carried a lot with them) and shelter.

Guests were always welcomed, as Odysseus was in the Phaeacian palace. This was a strong tradition, almost a law, in ancient times. When a guest arrived he was taken into the main hall, where a servant brought him a basin and jug to wash. Another servant put a table with food in front of him and no one asked him any questions about himself until he had eaten. As long as he wished to stay he was treated like a member of the household. When he left, his hosts helped him on his way. The Phaeacians took Odysseus all the way to Ithaca in one of their own ships.

Sport

The ancient Greeks were fond of many sports and games but the main sport, at least for noblemen, was hunting. It was more than entertainment and exercise. It was something good and necessary. It taught young men to be good fighters, it provided food and it was almost like a religious duty.

In Mycenaean times, and probably in Homer's time too, lions and panthers still lived in Greece. Men also hunted deer, hares and wild sheep called mouflon (still found in Cyprus). To kill them a hunter had to be skilful, but to kill a wild boar, the most common quarry, he had to be brave as well. Odysseus had a scar on his right thigh made by a boar he had hunted as a boy. Men hunted on foot, with the help of hounds (probably greyhounds). These hounds were treasured and often lived in the house as pets. When Odysseus returned to Ithaca in disguise no one recognised him except his old hound Argus, who wagged his tail feebly and then died. Different dogs, savage creatures like mastiffs, were kept to guard the flocks against wolves.

In the *Odyssey* dogs are described with affection. But in the *Iliad* they are described as unpleasant animals. This is one reason for thinking that the 'Homer' who wrote the *Odyssey* was a different person from the 'Homer' of the *Iliad*. While Odysseus was a guest of the king of the Phaeacians he watched the Phaeacian Games, in which young noblemen took part. The events included running races, jumping, throwing the discus, wrestling and boxing. One of the competitors persuaded Odysseus to take part in the discus. (Guess who won!)

This is the oldest description of an athletics meeting we have. However, such games were not new to the people who listened to Homer's stories. The first Olympic Games, in which Greeks from all over the country took part, were held in 776 BC, and every four years after that. The winners received a branch of wild olive, which meant as much to them as a gold medal does to our own Olympic champions.

The *Odyssey* also contains the first description of a ball game. It is played by Nausicaa and her maids on the beach, and was probably a simple game of catch. However, people were certainly playing with balls at a much earlier time. Some balls made of wood or of feathers covered with leather have been found in Egypt which are over 4000 years old.

Kirk Douglas played Odysseus in the film Ulysses.

If you go on a very long journey and it turns out to be a very difficult journey too, you might say afterwards, 'Oh, that was a real odyssey!' The word has become part of our language.

The *Odyssey* was written at the very beginning of European civilisation, nearly 3000 years ago, yet it is still part of our mental luggage like the story of Adam and Eve or the story of Cinderella. Odysseus, or Ulysses as he is often called, has always been with us. In a book about politics written in the reign of Henry VIII (1509–47) Odysseus is quoted as a good model for kings to copy. Odysseus appears in a play by Shakespeare (*Troilus and Cressida*). A seventeenth-century French author wrote a book criticising Odysseus and accusing him of neglecting his wife and family.

The Star Trek *series was inspired by the tales of the wandering Odysseus.*

Painters and writers have always found inspiration in the story of Odysseus and in their different ways they have added to the Odysseus legend. Writers of every century produced new translations of Homer's works. The Wedgwood pottery produced a china figure of Odysseus. Tennyson wrote a long poem about him after his return to Ithaca which contains the famous line summing up the sort of character that Odysseus was:

To strive, to seek, to fight, and not to yield.

In the twentieth century Odysseus has appeared in a film (played by Kirk Douglas) and in a long poem by Nikos Kazantzakis, a modern Greek poet. The *Odyssey* also inspired one of the most famous novels of this century, James Joyce's *Ulysses.*

In Joyce's book Odysseus becomes an Irishman, Leopold Bloom, wandering through Dublin, and the episodes of the story are roughly based on incidents in the *Odyssey* (for example, the Land of the Lotus Eaters becomes a Turkish Bath).

In Joyce's novel the Odysseus character is not much of a hero, though he has his moments of heroism. He is an Odysseus brought up to date, a man more typical of our civilisation than that of Ancient Greece. And there, perhaps, is the explanation for the continuing interest in Odysseus. He may be a king, a great warrior and a friend of the gods, but he is also an ordinary man, trying as best he can to deal with dangers and disappointments as all human beings must learn to do. Odysseus is not just a superhero. He is rather like us.

'Ulysses and the Sirens' by Herbert J. Draper (1864–1920).

One of the American moon spacecraft was called 'Odyssey'.

'James Joyce's Dance'
- a drawing of the author of Ulysses by Desmond Havensworth.

Index

Published by BBC Educational Publishing, Woodlands, 80 Wood Lane, London W12 0TT

First published 1990
Reprinted 1992, 1993

© 1990 Neil Grant/BBC Education

Paperback ISBN: 0 563 34415 6
Hardback ISBN: 0 563 34414 8

Printed in Great Britain by BPCC Paulton Books Limited
Typeset by Ace Filmsetting, England
Origination by Dot Gradations, England.

Picture credits
P7t Michael Holford, bl C. M. Dixon, br The Ancient Art & Architecture Collection; **p8** The Mansell Collection; **p9b** C. M. Dixon; **p11tr** Batsford BT Ltd; **p13** Michael Holford; **p14** Michael Holford; **p21** Michael Holford; **p22t** Penguin Books Ltd, b Jane Burton/Bruce Coleman Ltd; **p24** Erich Lessing/John Hillelson Agency; **p25** Ancient Art & Architecture Collection; **p27** C. M. Dixon; **p28** Batsford BT Ltd; **p30bl** Michael Holford; **ps31, 32, 34, 35** Batsford BT Ltd; **p36** Michael Holford; **p39tr** Hans Reinhard/Bruce Coleman Ltd; **p41br** Hackenberg/Zefa, tl C. M. Dixon; **p43** Ancient Art & Architecture Collection; **p44–45** Kobal Collection; **p46** Ferens Art Gallery, Hull/ Richmond & Riggs Photography; **p47tr** NASA/Science Photo Library, bl Humanities Research Center, The University of Texas at Austin.

Picture Research by Joanne King